Lady Lovely Locks

AND THE PIXIETAILS

Silkypup Saves the Day

By Kristin Brown
Illustrated by Pat Paris

A Golden Book · New York
Western Publishing Company, Inc., Racine, Wisconsin 53404

One beautiful spring morning Lady LovelyLocks and Silkypup were walking down the path to Pixietail Park. Pixietails sparkled and glistened above Lady LovelyLocks's hair. Other Pixietails chattered and bounced behind Silkypup, making up tongue twisters and jokes as they went.

"Remember, Silkypup," Lady LovelyLocks said as they came into the park, "you must always watch out for Duchess RavenWaves. She wants to rule LovelyLocks. She'll try anything, so we must be on our guard."

Silkypup barked to show that she understood, and then she ran off to play. Her special Pixietail friends did not follow her as usual, for they were very busy making up the funniest little rhymes that the Kingdom of LovelyLocks had ever heard.

   While Silkypup was chasing butterflies in the
Kingdom of LovelyLocks, Duchess RavenWaves was
deep in the heart of Tangleland, planning and
scheming.
   The duchess was busily plotting to steal Lady
LovelyLocks's comb. "Surely that is the secret of her
power," the duchess muttered.

Duchess RavenWaves covered her face with a dark veil. Then she climbed onto the back of her horse and galloped through the tangled brush toward the Kingdom of LovelyLocks.

She stopped at the edge of Pixietail Park and tied her horse to a tree. Then she peered through the leaves and watched and waited until the time was right.

Silkypup had spent the entire morning trying to find someone to play with. But everyone seemed to have something else to do!

Silkypup ran over to Pixiesparkle and jumped up and down. But Pixiesparkle was too busy chasing the sparkles of light that bounced off Pixietail Pond.

"I can't play now," Pixiesparkle said kindly. "Maybe a little later."

Silkypup ran across the park to Maiden CurlyCrown,
and she sat down and blinked her eyes.

"I'm sorry, Silkypup," Maiden CurlyCrown said softly,
"but I have ten more fern leaves to curl before Pixiecurl's
birthday bouquet is ready."

Silkypup stood up sadly and went to find Silkymane.
Silkymane was busy playing tag with Pixieshine.
Silkypup barked a few times, but Silkymane didn't even
notice her.

Then Silkypup ran over to Maiden FairHair. Maiden FairHair was busy waving the silk willow trees. She didn't look up when Silkypup barked.

Poor Silkypup decided to take a nap. She lay down in the grass and closed her eyes.

When she opened her eyes again, everyone was still busy.

Pixiesparkle was still chasing sparkles.

Maiden CurlyCrown was still curling fern leaves.

Silkymane was still chasing Pixieshine.

Maiden FairHair was still waving the silk willow trees.

Silkypup ran to the other side of the park. She saw Lady LovelyLocks resting against a tree, combing her hair. Magical sparkles made her hair glisten in the sunshine.

As Silkypup watched, a veiled lady sneaked out of the woods. She crept up behind Lady LovelyLocks.

Silkypup stood up and barked softly.

The mysterious lady stopped and looked around. No one else seemed to have noticed Silkypup's bark.

"Go away, you silly little dog," the mysterious lady muttered. She moved closer to Lady LovelyLocks.

Silkypup remembered what Lady LovelyLocks had told her. She realized that the mysterious lady was Duchess RavenWaves! Silkypup ran for help. She barked louder and louder.

Everyone stopped doing what they were doing.
Pixiesparkle stopped chasing sparkles.
Maiden CurlyCrown stopped curling fern leaves.
Silkymane stopped chasing Pixieshine.
Maiden FairHair stopped waving the silk willow trees.
Everyone came running to Silkypup.

"What's the matter, Silkypup?" asked Maiden CurlyCrown.

Silkypup led them quietly near the tree where Lady LovelyLocks was sitting. They all hid behind a bush and watched.

The duchess held her hand over Lady LovelyLocks's head. She carefully stretched out her fingers to grab the comb.

Maiden CurlyCrown, Maiden FairHair, and the Pixietails hurried toward Lady LovelyLocks. The duchess was just about to snatch the comb.

Silkypup raced straight toward the duchess. She grabbed the end of her black veil in her teeth. She pulled and pulled until the black veil was on the ground.

"Leave me alone, you bad puppy!" yelled Duchess RavenWaves.

"Duchess RavenWaves! I should have known!" said Maiden CurlyCrown.

Lady LovelyLocks had been surprised by all the noise. "What's going on?" she asked.

Silkypup tugged at Duchess RavenWaves's dress until the duchess dropped the comb and fell backward. When the duchess was on the ground, Silkypup sat on her.

"Why, Duchess RavenWaves!" said Lady LovelyLocks, picking up her comb. "Why would you want to take my comb?"

"It's the secret of your power," Duchess RavenWaves growled. "And I'll get my hands on it yet!"

Lady LovelyLocks turned to Silkypup. "Thank you, Silkypup," she said.

"Hurray for Silkypup!" everyone shouted.

Silkypup got so excited that she jumped up and ran toward her friends. The duchess saw her chance to escape. She scrambled to her feet, leapt onto her horse, and sped away.

"We must stop her!" Maiden FairHair exclaimed.

"No," said Lady LovelyLocks. "Let her go. We can never really stop the duchess until she understands that my power comes from kindness and goodness. It cannot be found in my comb or my hair, or in any other outward signs of beauty. When she learns that, she will find beauty and happiness of her own."

The Pixietails hurried over to Silkypup. "Because you saved the day," they said, "we are going to give you a present. It's a special little poem that we've been working on all morning." They all recited:

"Silkypup, Silkypup, so loyal and true,
Hero for the day, and we thank you!"

Silkypup barked her thank-you bark. She was everyone's special friend for the day, and her friends played all her favorite games with her through the sunny afternoon.